The Loudness of Sam

Story and pictures by James Proimos

HARCOURT BRACE & COMPANY
San Diego   New York   London

For Sally and Jim

Library of Congress Cataloging-in-Publication Data
Proimos, James.
The Loudness of Sam/story and pictures by James Proimos.
p.   cm.
Summary: A young boy who has always been allowed to express his feelings
as loudly as he wants teaches his citified aunt to do the same.
ISBN 0-15-202087-X
[I. Emotions—Fiction.   II. Aunts—Fiction.]   I. Title.
PZ7.P9432Lo   1999
[E]—dc21   98-29884

First edition
A C E F D B
Printed in Mexico

The illustrations in this book were first drawn with a pen,
then colorized in Adobe Photoshop.
The display type was set in Sitcom.
The text type was set in Goudy Old Style.
Color separations by Bright Arts Ltd., Hong Kong
Printed and bound by RR Donnelley & Sons, Reynosa, Mexico
This book was printed on totally chlorine-free Nymolla Matte Art paper.
Production supervision by Stanley Redfern and Ginger Boyer
Designed by Kaelin Chappell and James Proimos

When Sam came into this world, the doctor slapped him on the bottom. Because that is what doctors do.

And Sam cried **loudly**. Because that is what babies do.

Sam's
parents
wrapped
him
in a
quilt
made
of
love . . .

and drove him in a car made for three . . .

to a home that had been awaiting his arrival for a long, long time.

THE HOUSE HAD A ROOM FILLED WITH BALLS,

A TRAMPOLINE ROOM,

A ROOM WITH A SUPER TELESCOPE,

A ROOM FILLED WITH SQUISHY STUFF,

AND A ROOM FOR LISTENING TO HIS PARENTS' HUGE COLLECTION OF RECORDED SOUNDS.

When Sam was
gently placed into his crib,
he cried his eyes out.
Because that is what babies do.

Well into his first year,
Sam cried whenever he needed
one thing or another.

And when Sam cried,
Sam cried **loudly**.

On his first birthday,
his parents gave him a present.

When the present quacked,
Sam laughed.

And when Sam laughed,
Sam laughed **loudly**.

Sam's parents loved every sound he made.

They never, ever shushed him
for laughing **loudly**
when his heart was happy.

They never, ever hushed him
for crying **loudly**
when he needed comfort.

Not when he was three . . .

not when he was seven . . .

not even when he was older than that.

Sam had a wonderful life.

One day Sam got a letter from his aunt Tillie.

Dear Sam,

I have heard so much about you.
I would be honored if you would come visit me in the big city.
Will you?

Sincerely,
Aunt Tillie

He sent her one back.

Even though he was only going to be gone for a few days, Sam's parents cried like babies the day Aunt Tillie came to pick him up.

When Sam got to the big city,
he was amazed.

There were so many glad things
to make him laugh.

And so many sad things
that brought tears to his eyes.

A DUCK MADE OF BALLOONS

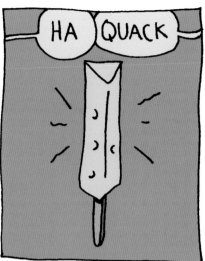

CHEESE ON A STICK

GARBAGE IN THE STREETS

BUNNY SLIPPERS

A LOST & HUNGRY KITTY

A SILLY HAT

A DAD SHUSHING HIS KID

UNDERWEAR MODELS

A DOG WITH GAS

But Sam noticed that no one seemed to pay attention to any of these sad or glad things.

No one cried **loudly**.

No one laughed **loudly**.

No one seemed to laugh or cry hardly at all.

Not even Aunt Tillie.

When Aunt Tillie took Sam to the library,
he cried **loudly**.

Everyone shushed Sam. Aunt Tillie said,
"Crying is for donkeys!"

When Aunt Tillie took Sam to the movies, he laughed **loudly**.

Everyone hushed Sam. Aunt Tillie said, "Laughing is for monkeys!"

When Aunt Tillie took Sam out to dinner,
he cried **loudly** once more.

Everyone shushed Sam. This time, Aunt Tillie
just looked at him curiously.

On the last day of Sam's visit,
something very strange happened.

When Aunt Tillie went out
to get the morning paper,
she looked up and saw a cloud that
looked like a funny nose and glasses.

She laughed **loudly**.

And when she read the sad story on the front page at breakfast, she cried **loudly**...

so loudly, she woke Sam.

Sam asked, "Why are you crying?"

"Well, suddenly, I don't seem able to keep the sadness or gladness inside of me. I'm not sure why," said Aunt Tillie.

Sam laughed **loudly**.

"Why are you laughing?" asked Aunt Tillie.

"Well, wouldn't I be foolish not to enjoy the things that make my heart happy?" said Sam.

Aunt Tillie laughed, too.

Just like some people catch a cold, Aunt Tillie had caught the Loudness of Sam.

When it was time to leave, Sam gave Aunt Tillie a present. She cried **loudly** because she knew she would miss Sam.

But when the present quacked, they both
laughed **loudly**.

In fact, Sam and Aunt Tillie didn't stop laughing until the very last star came out and Sam was back home again.